# SAM
# &
# DAVE
# DIG
# A
# HOLE

Mac Barnett

illustrated by

Jon Klassen

CANDLEWICK PRESS

On Monday Sam and Dave dug a hole.

"When should we stop digging?" asked Sam.

"We are on a mission," said Dave.

"We won't stop digging until we find

  something spectacular."

The hole got so deep that their heads were underground.
But they still had not found anything spectacular.
"We need to keep digging," said Dave.

So they kept digging.

They took a break.

Dave drank chocolate milk

out of a canteen.

Sam ate animal cookies he had wrapped

in their grandfather's kerchief.

"Maybe," said Dave,

"the problem is that we are

digging straight down."

"Yes," said Sam.

"That could be the problem."

"I think we should dig in

another direction," said Dave.

"Yes," said Sam.

"That is a good idea."

"I have a new idea," said Dave.

"Let's split up."

"Really?" said Sam.

"Just for a little while," said Dave.

"It will help our chances."

So Dave went one way,

and Sam went another.

But they did not find anything spectacular.
"Maybe we should go back to digging
straight down," said Dave.

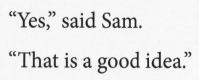

"Yes," said Sam.

"That is a good idea."

Sam and Dave ran out of chocolate milk.

But they kept digging.

They shared the last animal cookie.

But they kept digging.

After a while Sam sat down.

"Dave," he said, "I am tired.

I cannot dig anymore."

"I am tired too," said Dave.

"We should take a rest."

Sam and Dave fell asleep.

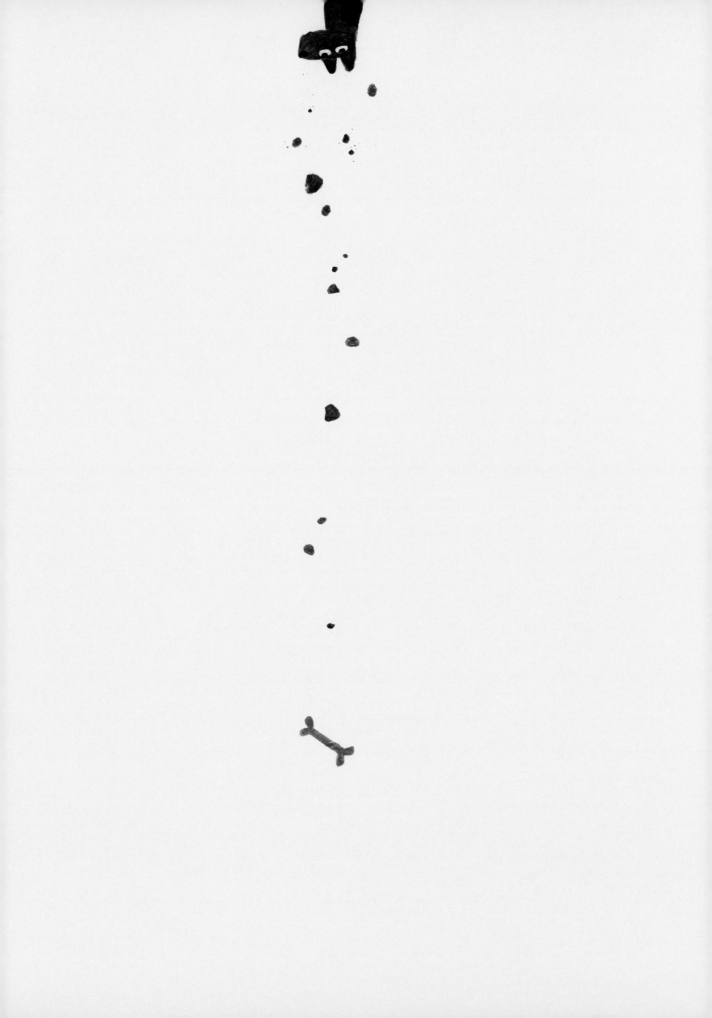

Then Sam and Dave were falling.

Sam and Dave fell down,



down,



down,

until they landed in the soft dirt.

"Well," said Sam.

"Well," said Dave.

"That was pretty spectacular."

And they went inside

for chocolate milk and animal cookies.